Higgledy Piggledy

The hen who loved to dance

For Joshua, who also loves to dance,
and for my parents, Sondra and Mayo
FS

To my nephew André
EM

First published in a special edition by HarperCollins Publishers in 1994
First hardback edition published by HarperCollins Publishers in 1995
First paperback edition published by HarperCollins Children's Books in 2015
This hardback edition published by HarperCollins Children's Books in 2016

HarperCollins Children's Books is a division of HarperCollins Publishers Ltd.

3 5 7 9 10 8 6 4 2

ISBN: 978-0-00-813946-9

Visit our website at: www.harpercollins.co.uk
Printed and bound in China

Higgledy Piggledy

The hen who loved to dance

Francesca Simon

Illustrated by Elisabeth Moseng

HarperCollins *Children's Books*

Higgledy-Piggledy didn't lay
eggs like her mother or crow
cock-a-doodle-do like her father.
Higgledy-Piggledy danced.

Hour after hour, day after day, Higgledy-Piggledy practiced her pirouettes,

twirling and whirling across the farmyard.

The other animals thought Higgledy-Piggledy
was a silly, lazy, good-for-nothing hen.
"Why don't you do something useful?"
said Calypso. "I catch mice."

"I pull the cart," said Festival.

"I give milk," said Lily.

"I make wool," said Delilah.

"I lay eggs," said Big Blanche.

"I provide down and feathers," said Dilly.

"I protect you all," said Towser.

Everyone looked at Higgledy-Piggledy.

"I dance," said Higgledy-Piggledy.

Even Higgledy-Piggledy's mother said there was no future in it. "Whoever heard of a dancing hen?"

But Higgledy-Piggledy just went on practicing her twirls and high-steps, trying to spin on one leg without falling over.

"Time you stopped dancing and started laying," said Calypso. "My Max is no older than you, and look what a good mouse-catcher he is."

"1-2-3, 1-2-3, 1-2-3," muttered Higgledy-Piggledy, waltzing into the duck pond.

One hot summer day Dilly started honking.
  "Help! Help! Help!"
  All the animals ran into the farmyard.
  "What is it? What's wrong?" asked Festival.
  "Max is in trouble!" shouted Dilly.

Max huddled at the top of the tall oak tree.

"Help!" meowed Max.

"Come down at once, Max," said Calypso.

But Max was too scared to move. "I can't," said Max. "It's too high. I'm stuck." And he started to cry.

"Don't worry, Max, I'll help you," said Festival,
and he pulled his cart.

"I'll help," said Lily,
and she brought milk.

"I'll help," said Delilah,
and she gave wool.

"I'll help," said Big Blanche,
and she laid an egg.

"I'll help," said Dilly, and she plucked a feather.

"I'll help," said Towser, and he barked.

"I'm slipping," said Max.

"Somebody do something!" screamed Calypso.

Just then Higgledy-Piggledy
pirouetted across the yard.

"Look at me! Look at me! Look at
me!" shrieked Higgledy-Piggledy. "I can do it!"

Around and around twirled Higgledy-Piggledy,
balancing gracefully on one leg. She looked wonderful.

Max forgot he was scared. Max forgot he was high up in the oak tree. Max wanted to dance, too. His paws began to move, and before he knew it he'd danced down the tree.

Then Higgledy-Piggledy and Max
glided around the farmyard together.
"That looks like fun," said Festival.
"I wish I could dance," said Lily.

"All together class. 1, 2, 3, twirl!"
said Higgledy-Piggledy.

"That's my girl," said Big Blanche proudly.